J.M. Barrie's
Peter Pan

Adapted by
Joeming Dunn

Illustrated by
Ben Dunn

magic
wagon

visit us at
www.abdopublishing.com

Published by Magic Wagon, a division of the ABDO Publishing Group, 8000 West 78th Street, Edina, Minnesota 55439. Copyright © 2008 by Abdo Consulting Group, Inc. International copyrights reserved in all countries. All rights reserved. No part of this book may be reproduced in any form without written permission from the publisher. Graphic Planet™ is a trademark and logo of Magic Wagon.

Printed in the United States of America, North Mankato, Minnesota.
012008   012011

Original novel by J.M. Barrie
Adapted by Joeming Dunn
Illustrated by Ben Dunn
Colored by Robby Bevard
Lettered by Joeming Dunn
Edited by Stephanie Hedlund
Interior layout and design by Antarctic Press
Cover art by Rod Espinosa
Cover design by Neil Klinepier

Library of Congress Cataloging-in-Publication Data

Dunn, Joeming W.
    Peter Pan / J.M. Barrie ; adapted by Joeming Dunn ; illustrated by Ben Dunn.
    p. cm. -- (Graphic classics)
    Includes bibliographical references.
    ISBN 978-1-60270-052-9
    1. Graphic novels. I. Dunn, Ben. II. Barrie, J.M. (James Matthew), 1860-1937. Peter Pan. III. Title.

PN6727.E86M63 2008
741.5'973--dc22

                           2007012070

TABLE of CONTENTS

Chapter 1 The Darlings

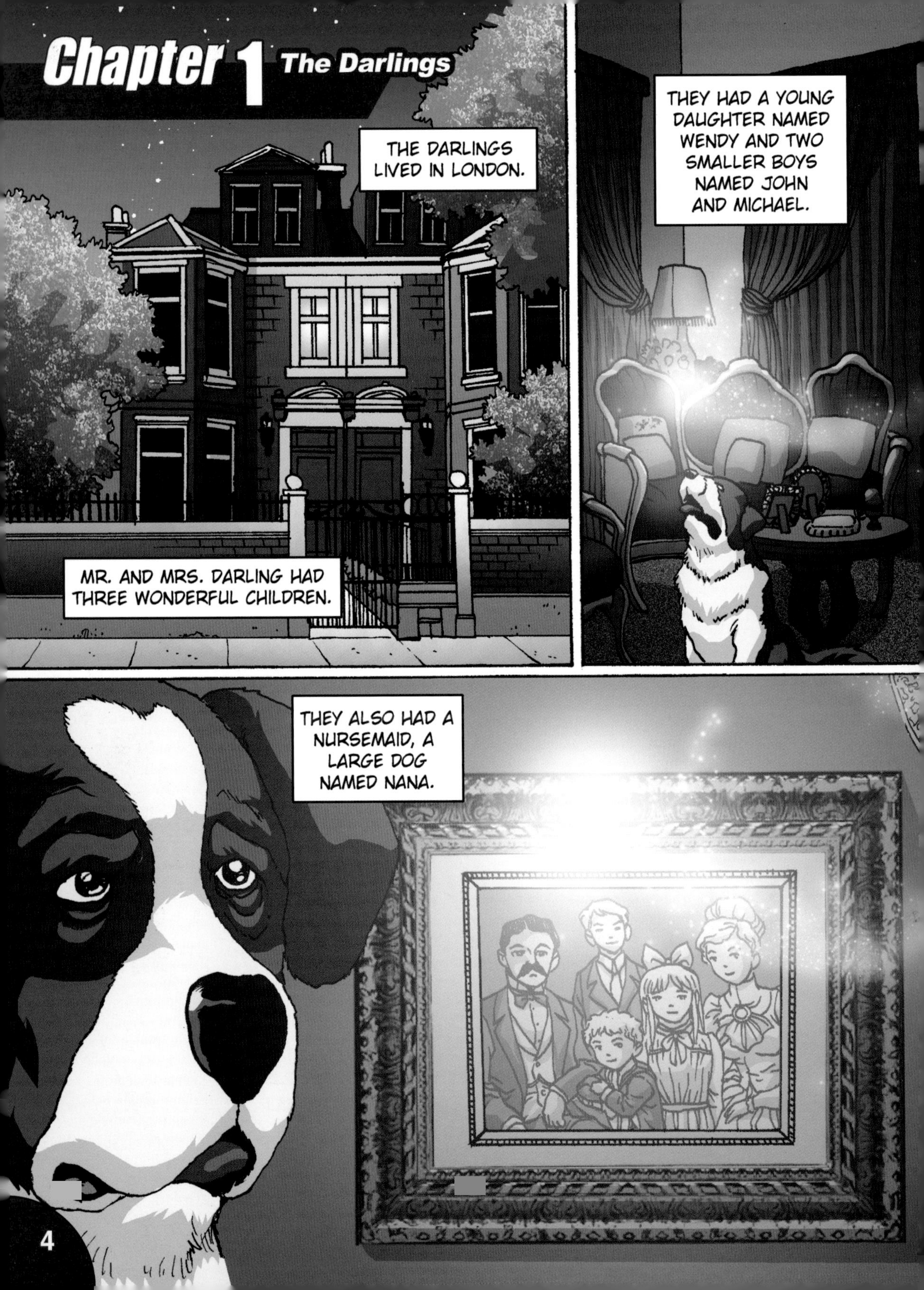
THE DARLINGS LIVED IN LONDON.
MR. AND MRS. DARLING HAD THREE WONDERFUL CHILDREN.
THEY HAD A YOUNG DAUGHTER NAMED WENDY AND TWO SMALLER BOYS NAMED JOHN AND MICHAEL.
THEY ALSO HAD A NURSEMAID, A LARGE DOG NAMED NANA.

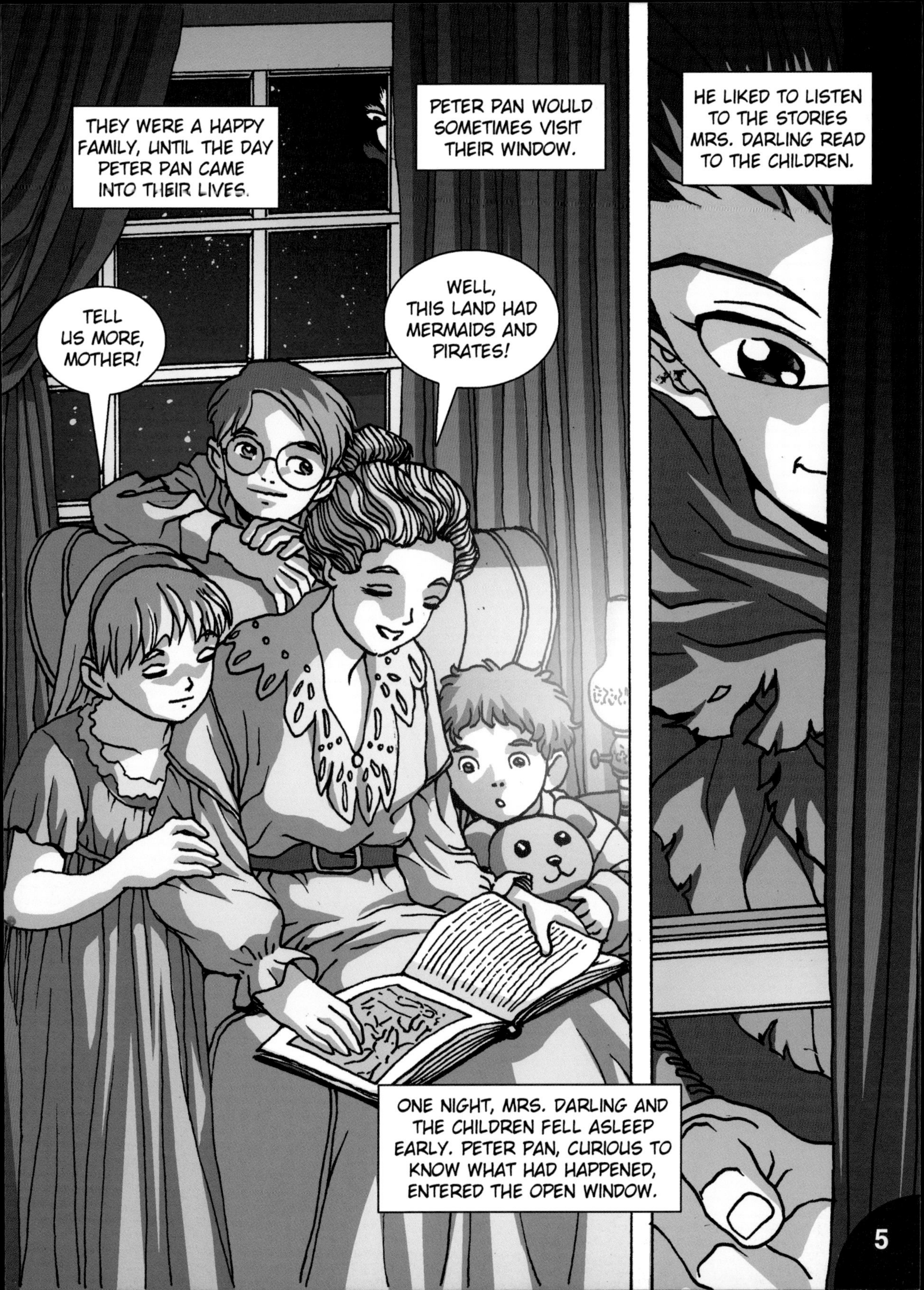
THEY WERE A HAPPY FAMILY, UNTIL THE DAY PETER PAN CAME INTO THEIR LIVES.
PETER PAN WOULD SOMETIMES VISIT THEIR WINDOW.
TELL US MORE, MOTHER!
WELL, THIS LAND HAD MERMAIDS AND PIRATES!
ONE NIGHT, MRS. DARLING AND THE CHILDREN FELL ASLEEP EARLY. PETER PAN, CURIOUS TO KNOW WHAT HAD HAPPENED, ENTERED THE OPEN WINDOW.
HE LIKED TO LISTEN TO THE STORIES MRS. DARLING READ TO THE CHILDREN.

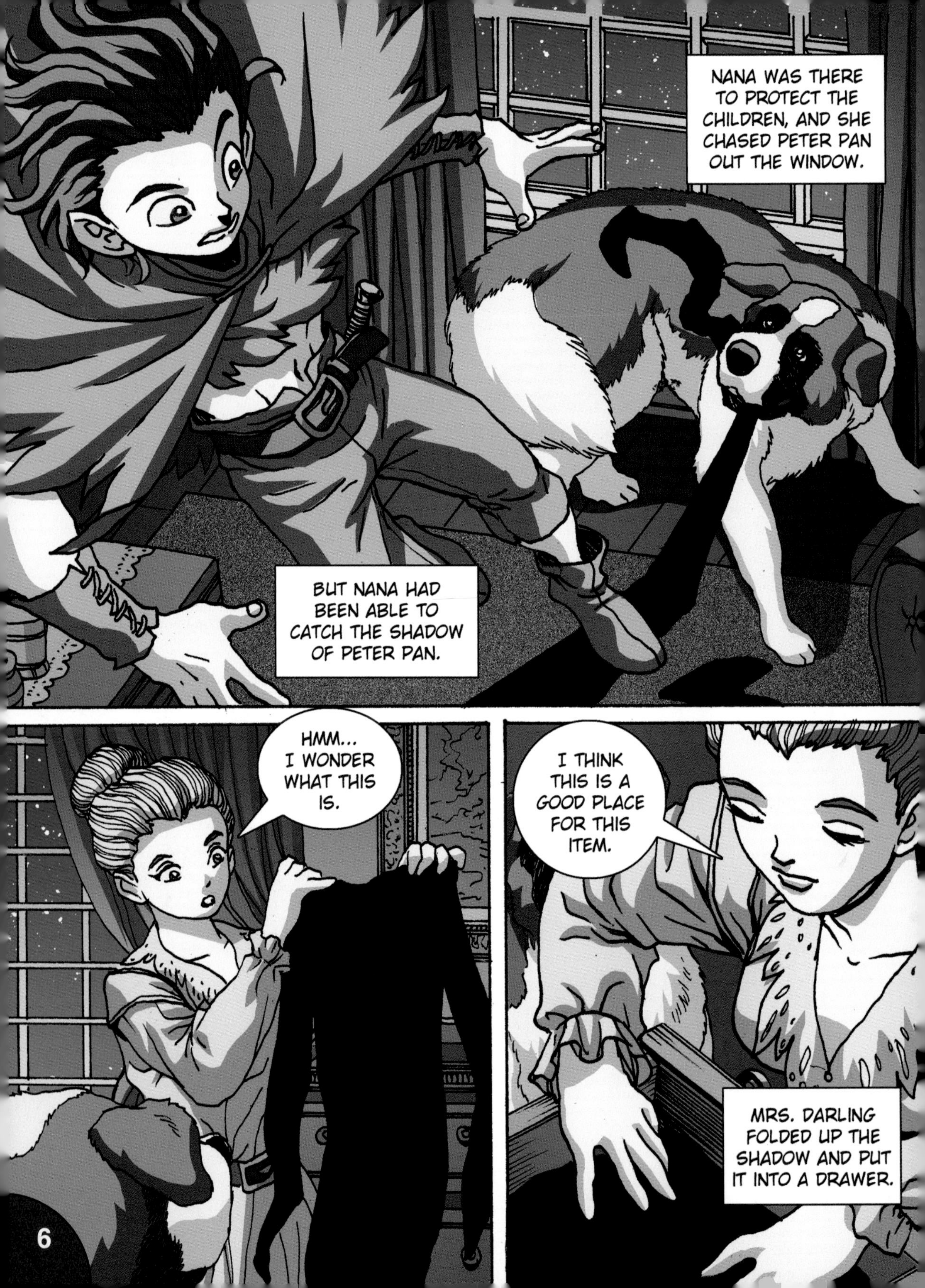
NANA WAS THERE TO PROTECT THE CHILDREN, AND SHE CHASED PETER PAN OUT THE WINDOW.
BUT NANA HAD BEEN ABLE TO CATCH THE SHADOW OF PETER PAN.
HMM... I WONDER WHAT THIS IS.
I THINK THIS IS A GOOD PLACE FOR THIS ITEM.
MRS. DARLING FOLDED UP THE SHADOW AND PUT IT INTO A DRAWER.

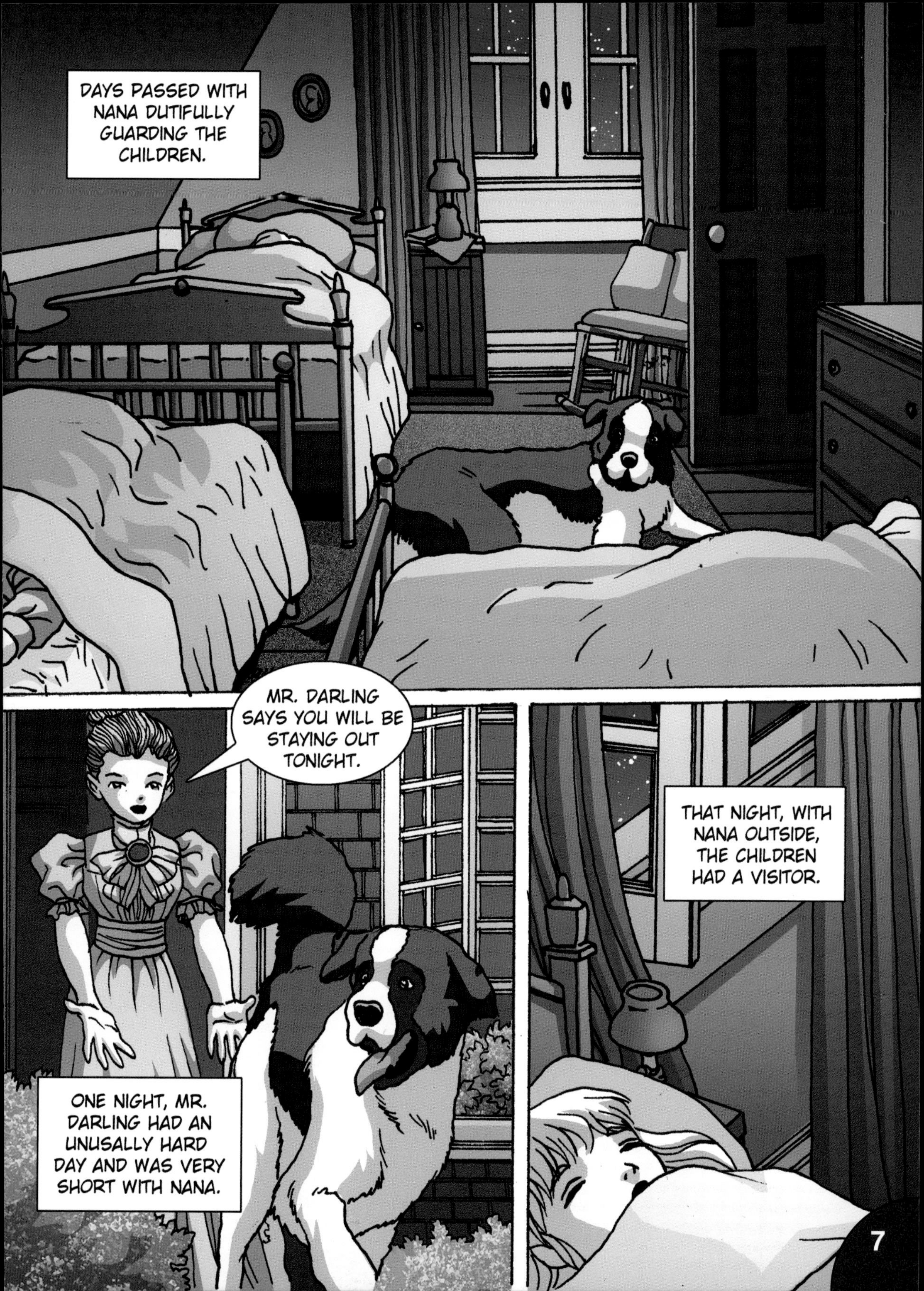
DAYS PASSED WITH NANA DUTIFULLY GUARDING THE CHILDREN.
MR. DARLING SAYS YOU WILL BE STAYING OUT TONIGHT.
ONE NIGHT, MR. DARLING HAD AN UNUSALLY HARD DAY AND WAS VERY SHORT WITH NANA.
THAT NIGHT, WITH NANA OUTSIDE, THE CHILDREN HAD A VISITOR.

Chapter 2 Peter's Shadow

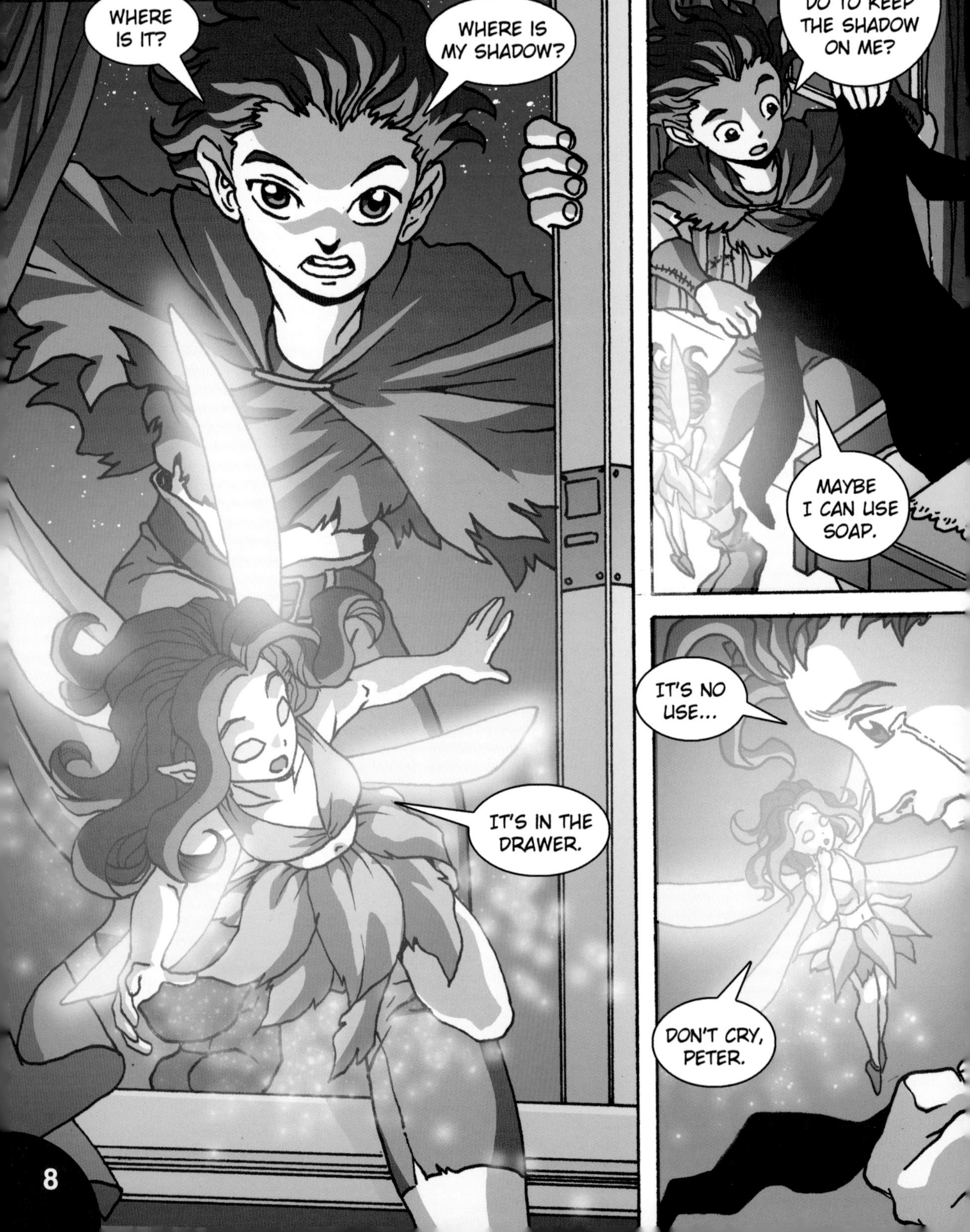

WHERE IS IT?
WHERE IS MY SHADOW?
IT'S IN THE DRAWER.
WHAT AM I GOING TO DO TO KEEP THE SHADOW ON ME?
MAYBE I CAN USE SOAP.
IT'S NO USE...
DON'T CRY, PETER.

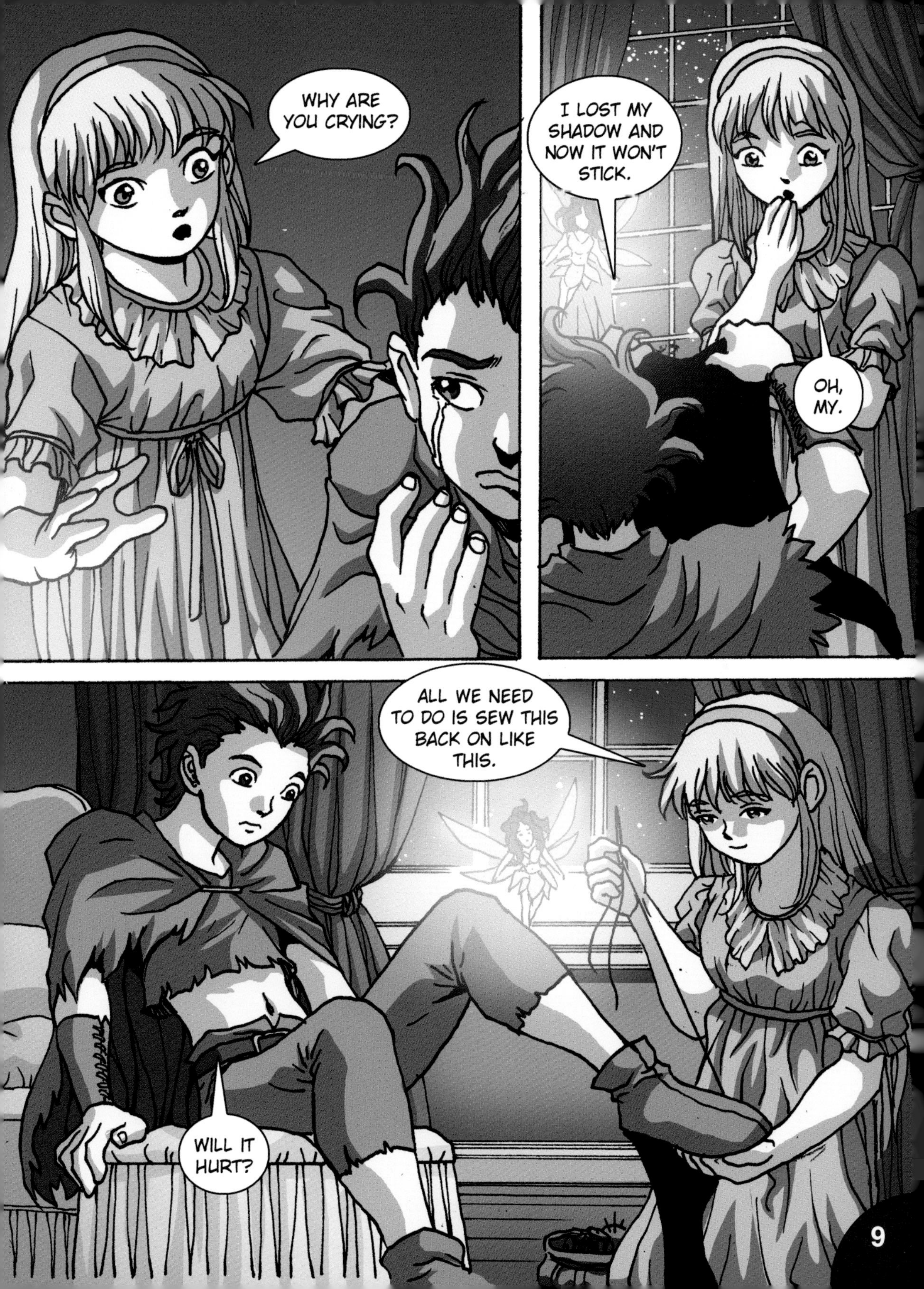
WHY ARE YOU CRYING?
I LOST MY SHADOW AND NOW IT WON'T STICK.
OH, MY.
ALL WE NEED TO DO IS SEW THIS BACK ON LIKE THIS.
WILL IT HURT?

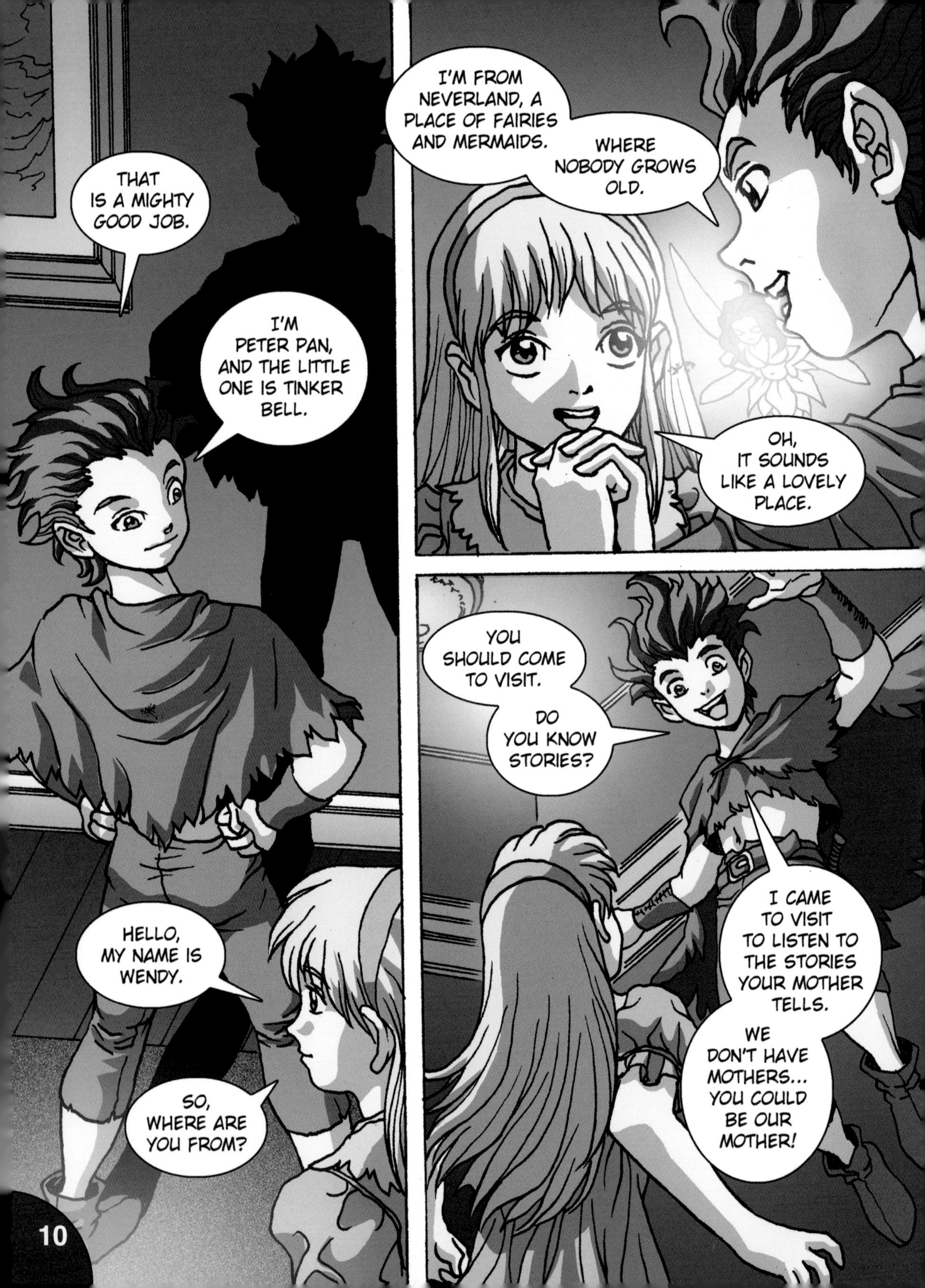
THAT IS A MIGHTY GOOD JOB.
I'M PETER PAN, AND THE LITTLE ONE IS TINKER BELL.
HELLO, MY NAME IS WENDY.
SO, WHERE ARE YOU FROM?
I'M FROM NEVERLAND, A PLACE OF FAIRIES AND MERMAIDS.
WHERE NOBODY GROWS OLD.
OH, IT SOUNDS LIKE A LOVELY PLACE.
YOU SHOULD COME TO VISIT.
DO YOU KNOW STORIES?
I CAME TO VISIT TO LISTEN TO THE STORIES YOUR MOTHER TELLS.
WE DON'T HAVE MOTHERS... YOU COULD BE OUR MOTHER!

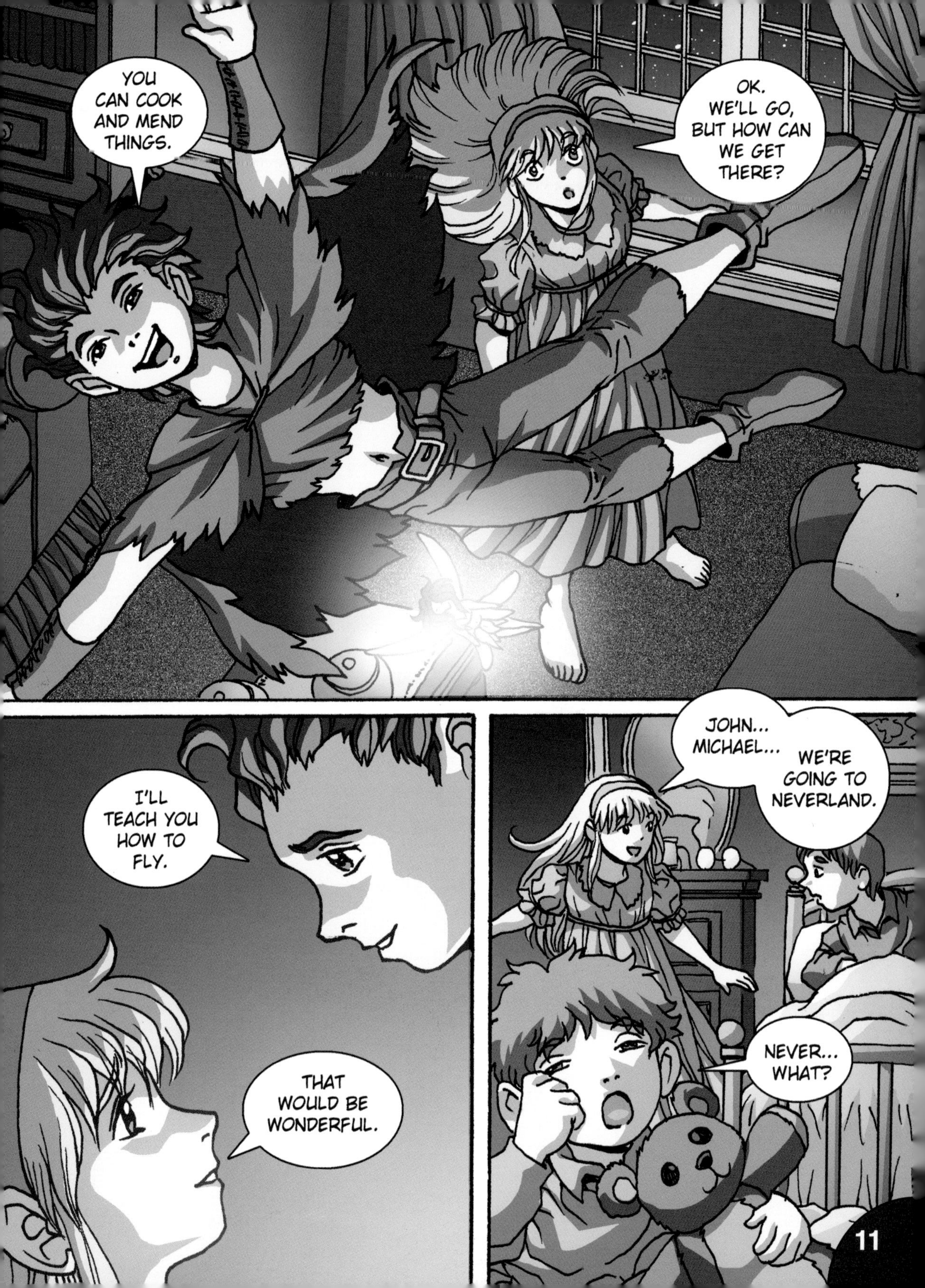
YOU CAN COOK AND MEND THINGS.
OK. WE'LL GO, BUT HOW CAN WE GET THERE?
I'LL TEACH YOU HOW TO FLY.
THAT WOULD BE WONDERFUL.
JOHN... MICHAEL...
WE'RE GOING TO NEVERLAND.
NEVER... WHAT?

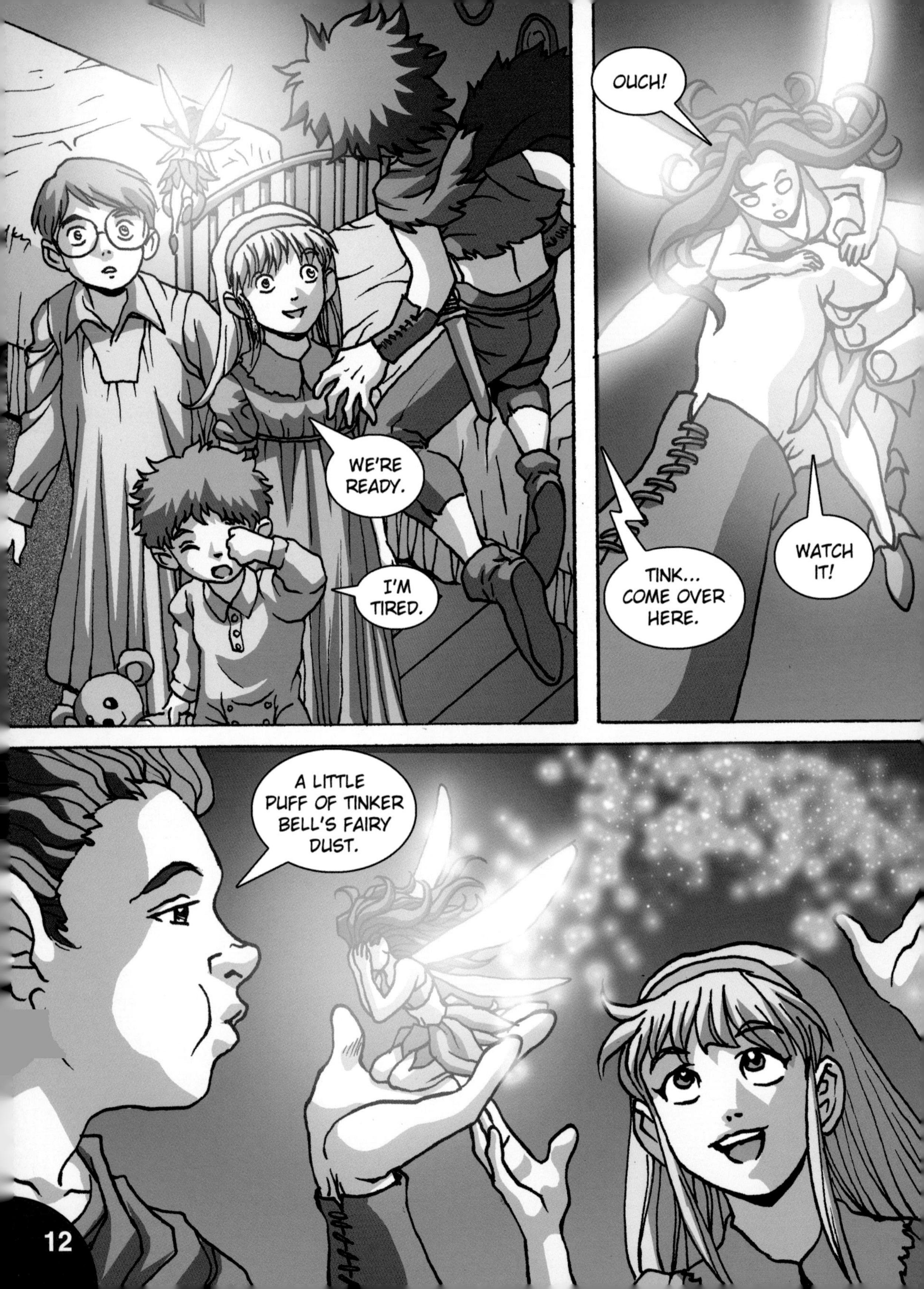
WE'RE READY.
I'M TIRED.
OUCH!
TINK... COME OVER HERE.
WATCH IT!
A LITTLE PUFF OF TINKER BELL'S FAIRY DUST.

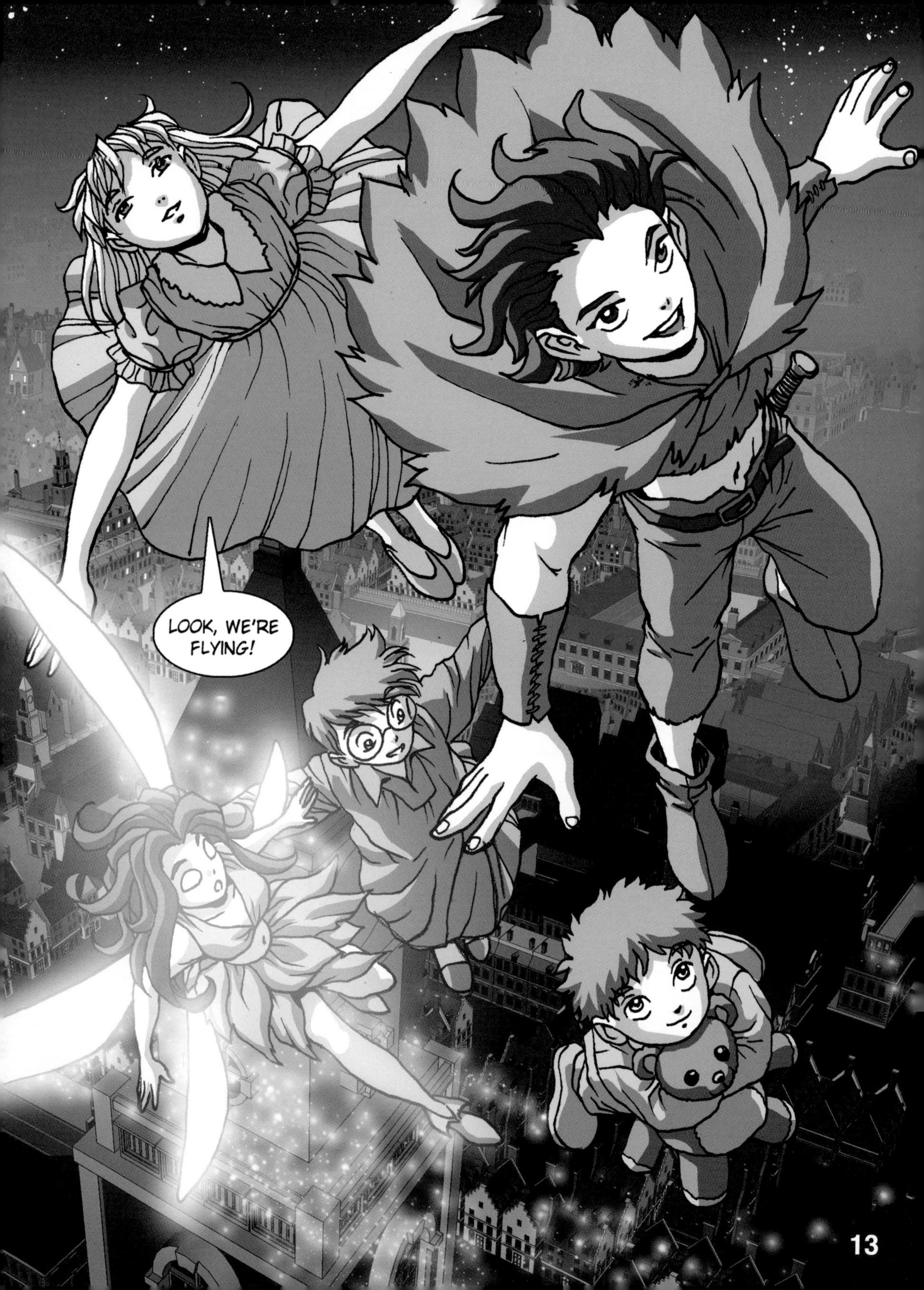
LOOK, WE'RE FLYING!

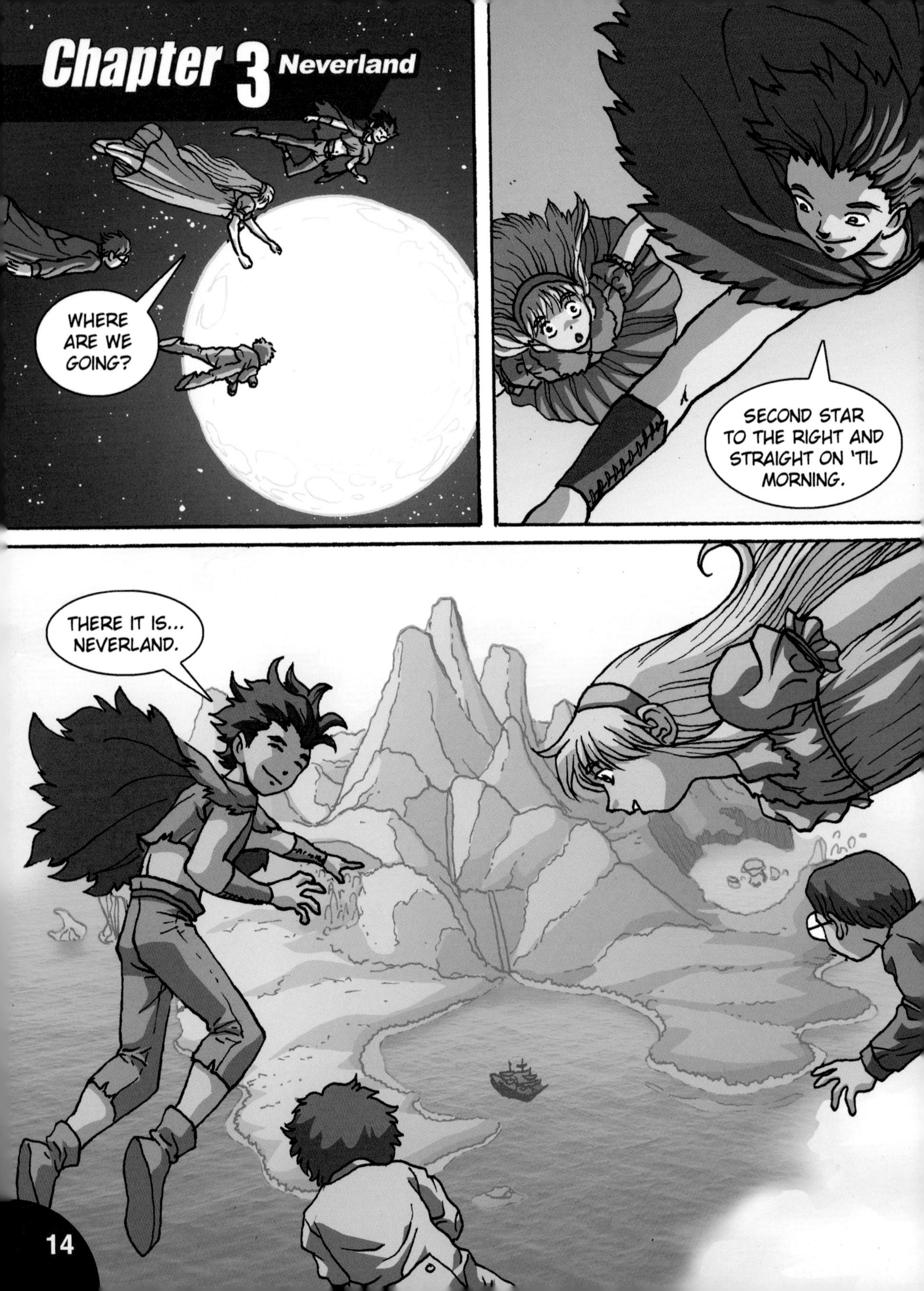
Chapter 3 Neverland
WHERE ARE WE GOING?
SECOND STAR TO THE RIGHT AND STRAIGHT ON 'TIL MORNING.
THERE IT IS... NEVERLAND.

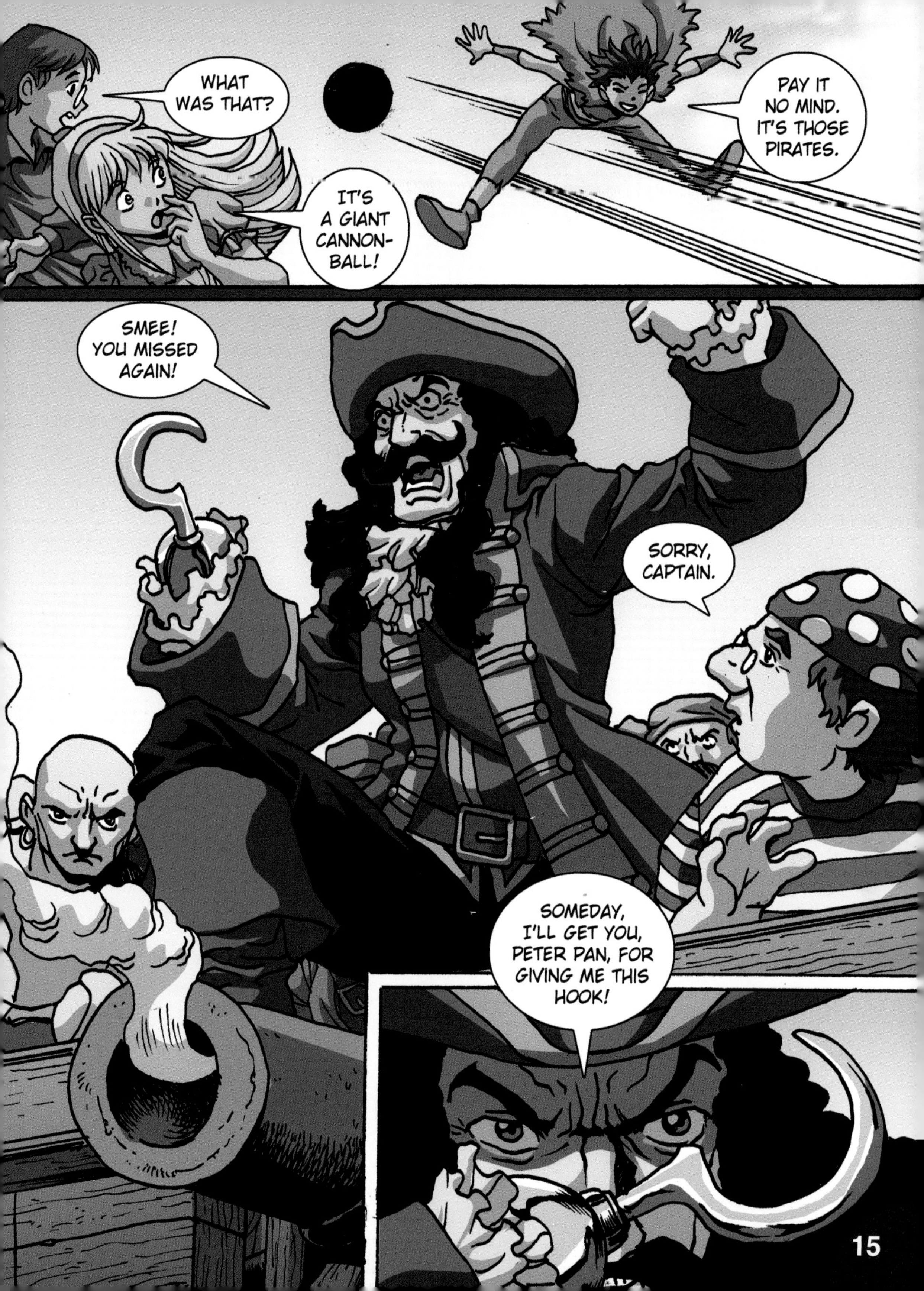
WHAT WAS THAT?
IT'S A GIANT CANNON-BALL!
PAY IT NO MIND. IT'S THOSE PIRATES.
SMEE! YOU MISSED AGAIN!
SORRY, CAPTAIN.
SOMEDAY, I'LL GET YOU, PETER PAN, FOR GIVING ME THIS HOOK!

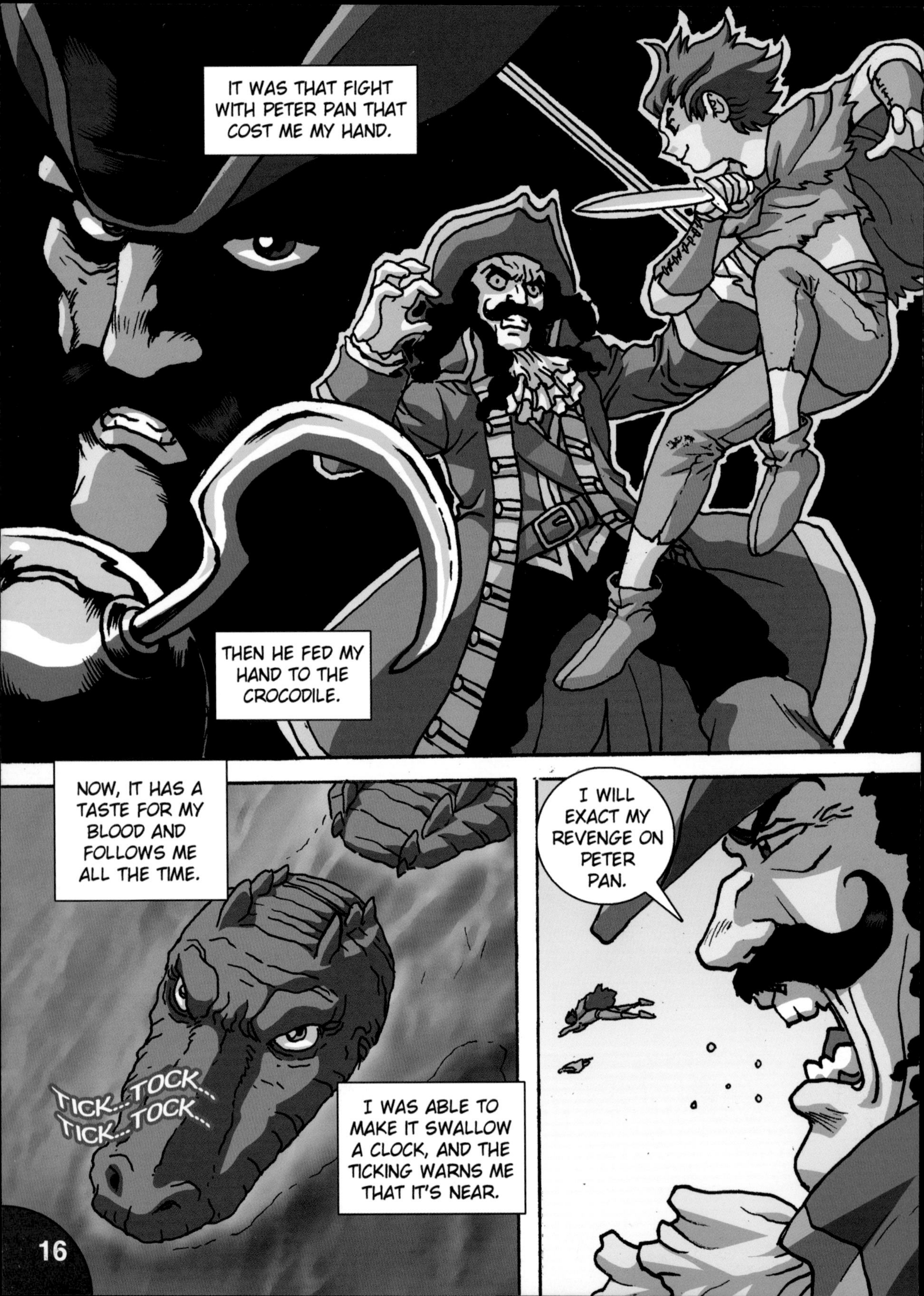
IT WAS THAT FIGHT WITH PETER PAN THAT COST ME MY HAND.
THEN HE FED MY HAND TO THE CROCODILE.
NOW, IT HAS A TASTE FOR MY BLOOD AND FOLLOWS ME ALL THE TIME.
TICK...TOCK... TICK...TOCK...
I WAS ABLE TO MAKE IT SWALLOW A CLOCK, AND THE TICKING WARNS ME THAT IT'S NEAR.
I WILL EXACT MY REVENGE ON PETER PAN.

Chapter 4 The Lost Boys

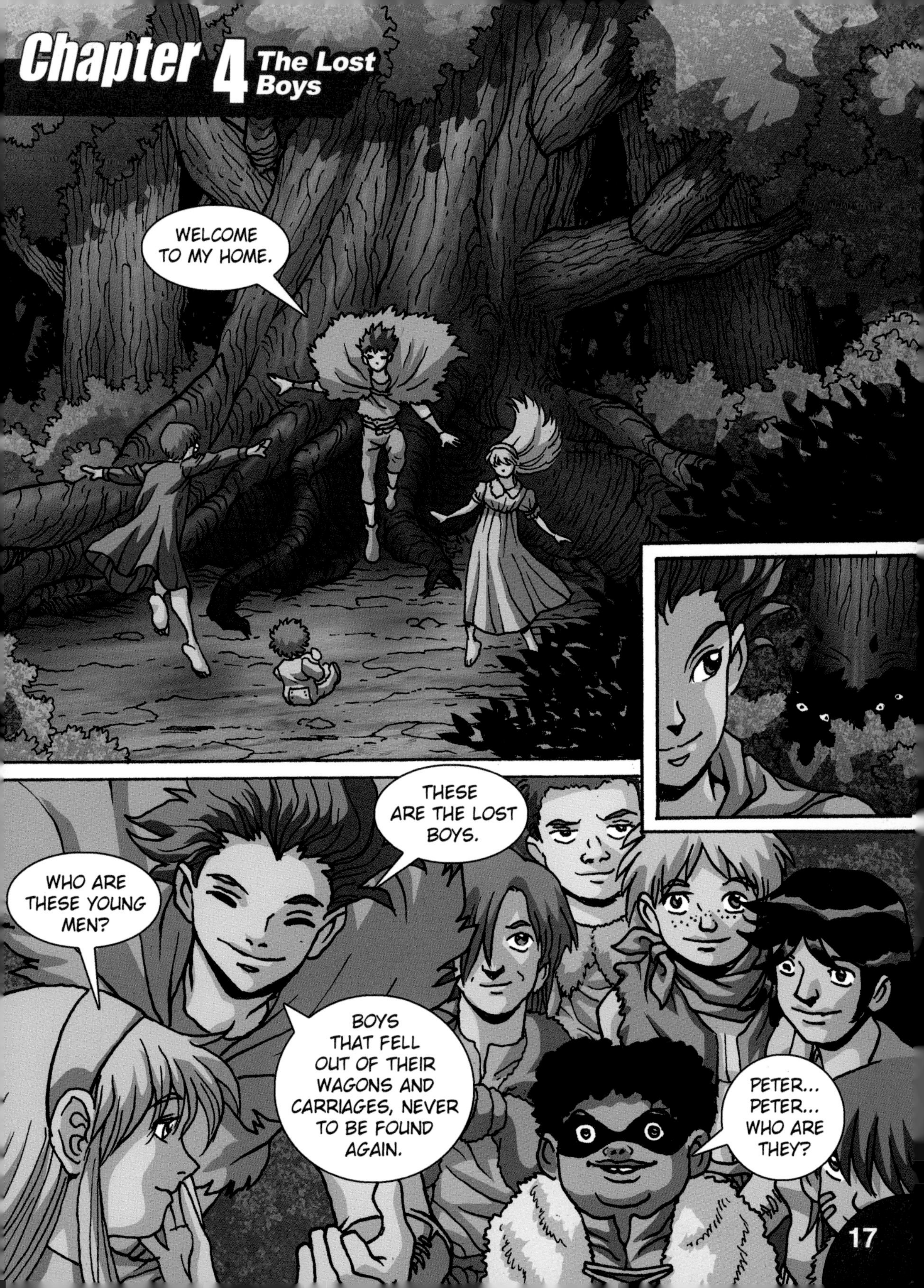
WELCOME TO MY HOME.
THESE ARE THE LOST BOYS.
WHO ARE THESE YOUNG MEN?
BOYS THAT FELL OUT OF THEIR WAGONS AND CARRIAGES, NEVER TO BE FOUND AGAIN.
PETER... PETER... WHO ARE THEY?

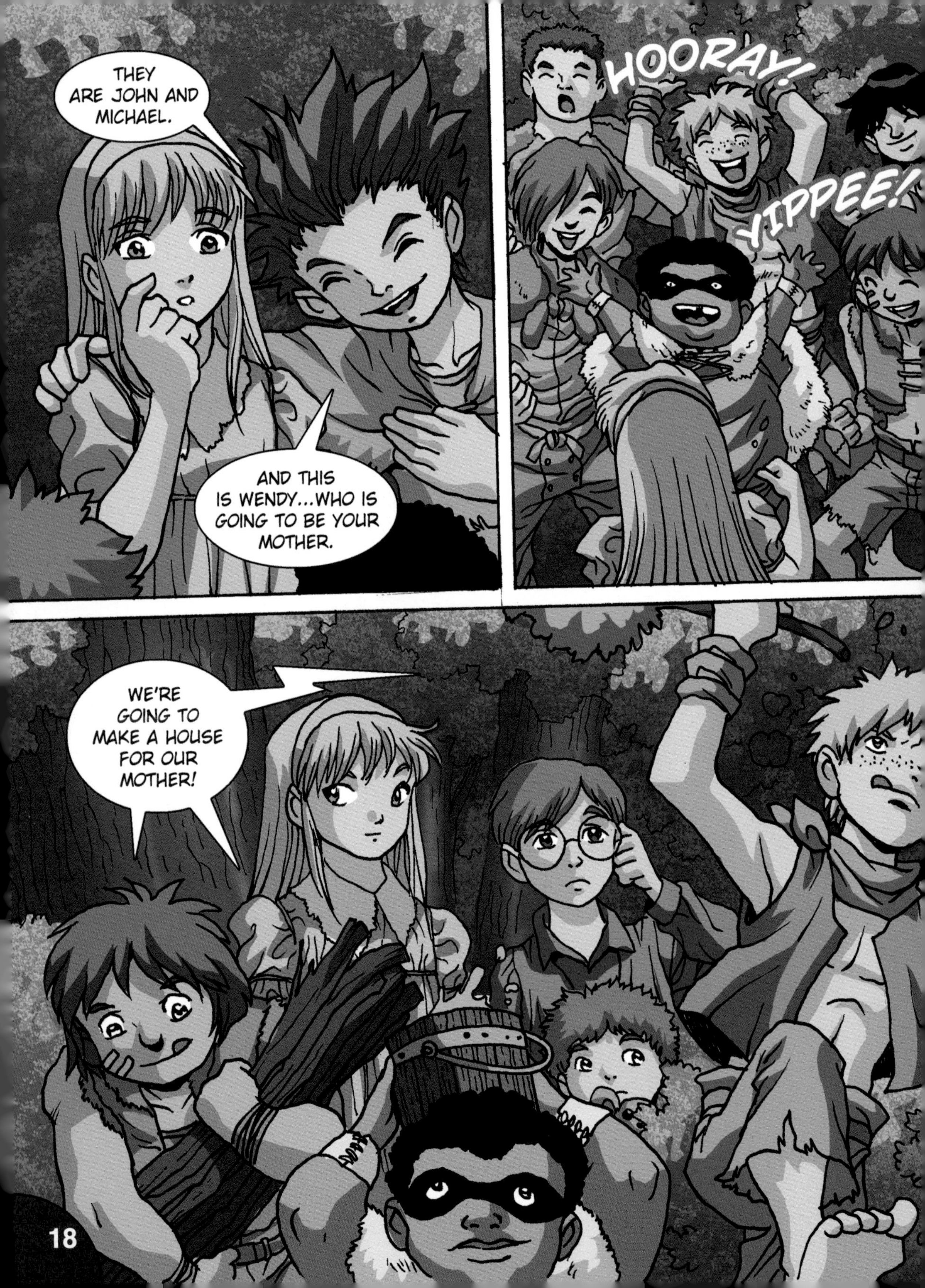
THEY ARE JOHN AND MICHAEL.
AND THIS IS WENDY...WHO IS GOING TO BE YOUR MOTHER.
HOORAY!
YIPPEE!
WE'RE GOING TO MAKE A HOUSE FOR OUR MOTHER!

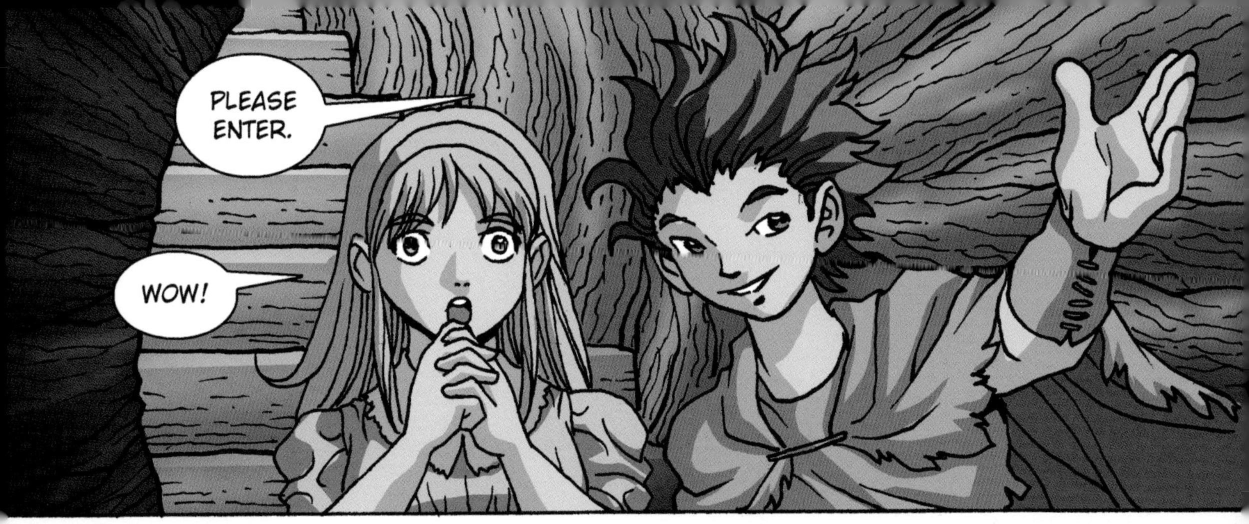
PLEASE ENTER.
WOW!

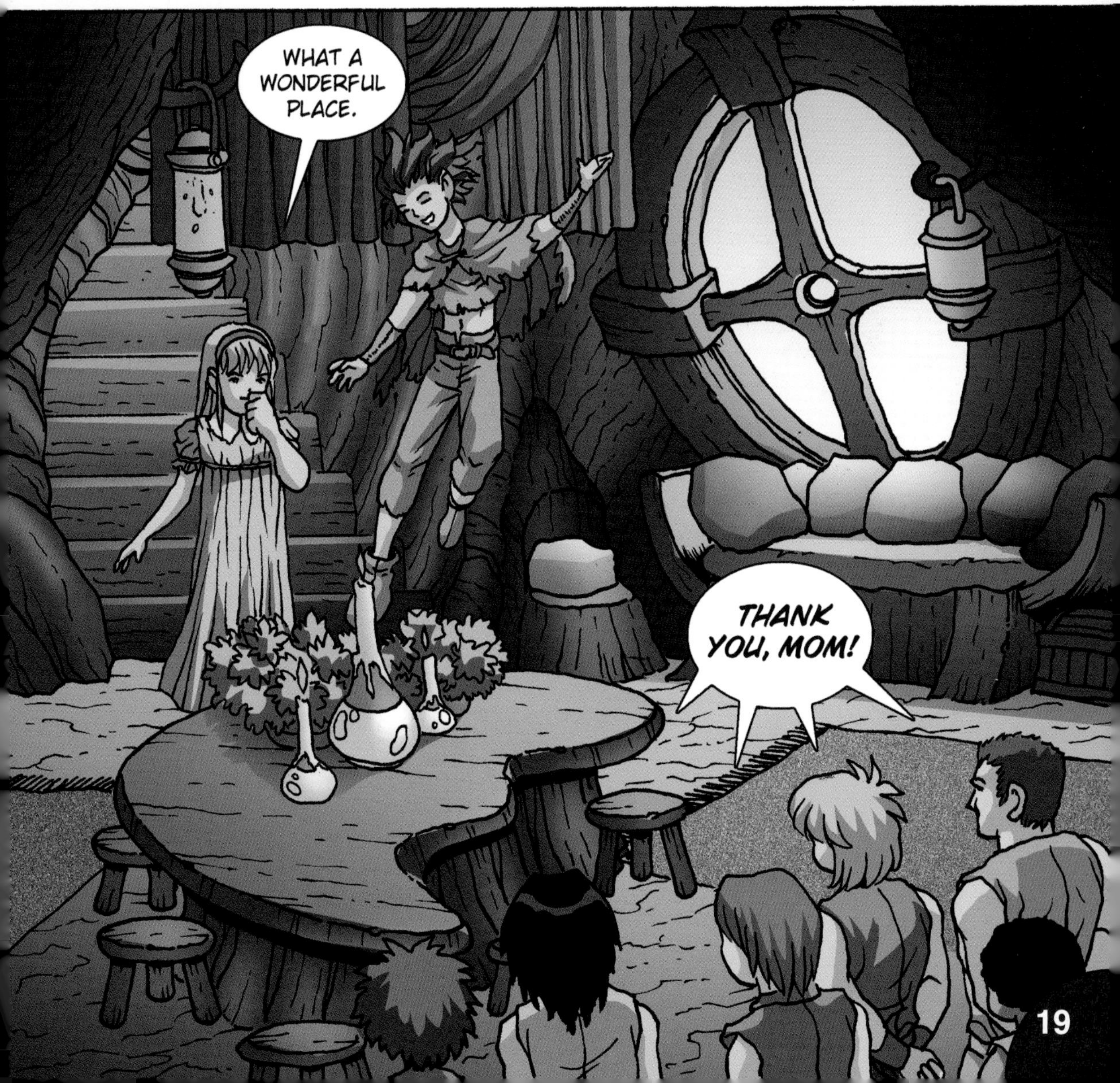
WHAT A WONDERFUL PLACE.
THANK YOU, MOM!

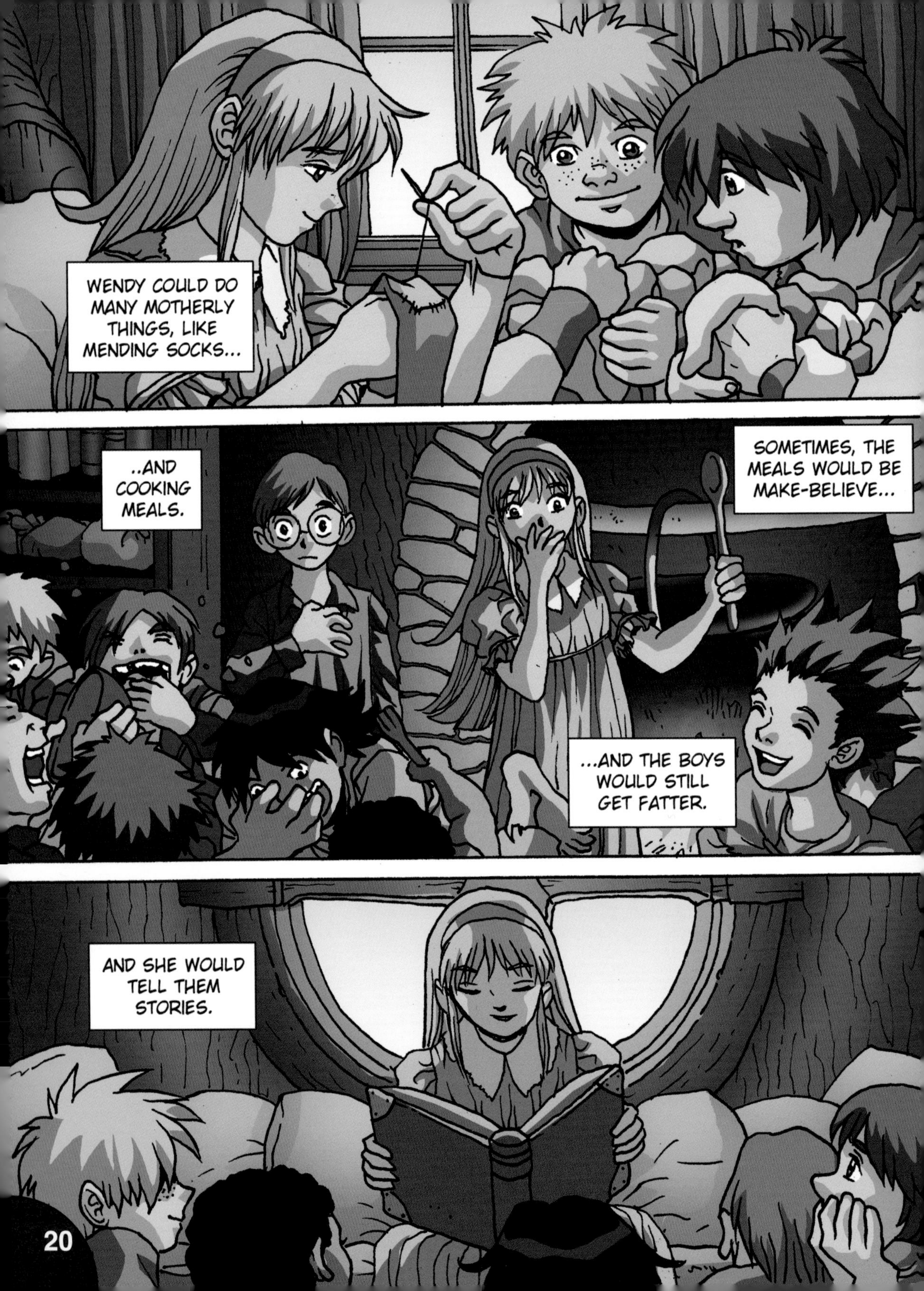
WENDY COULD DO MANY MOTHERLY THINGS, LIKE MENDING SOCKS...
..AND COOKING MEALS.
SOMETIMES, THE MEALS WOULD BE MAKE-BELIEVE...
...AND THE BOYS WOULD STILL GET FATTER.
AND SHE WOULD TELL THEM STORIES.

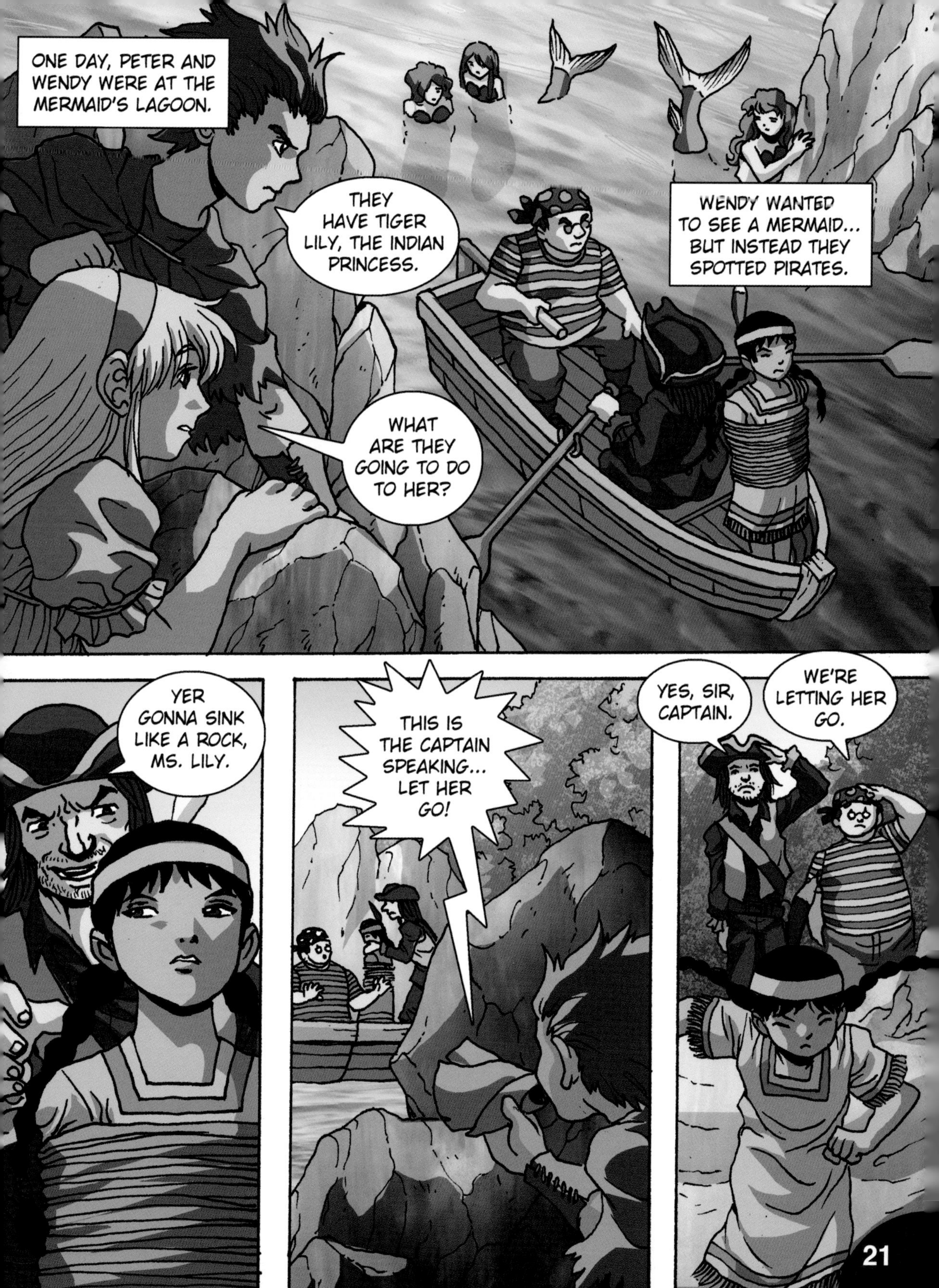

ONE DAY, PETER AND WENDY WERE AT THE MERMAID'S LAGOON.
THEY HAVE TIGER LILY, THE INDIAN PRINCESS.
WENDY WANTED TO SEE A MERMAID... BUT INSTEAD THEY SPOTTED PIRATES.
WHAT ARE THEY GOING TO DO TO HER?
YER GONNA SINK LIKE A ROCK, MS. LILY.
THIS IS THE CAPTAIN SPEAKING... LET HER GO!
WE'RE LETTING HER GO.
YES, SIR, CAPTAIN.

Chapter 5 Hook's Revenge

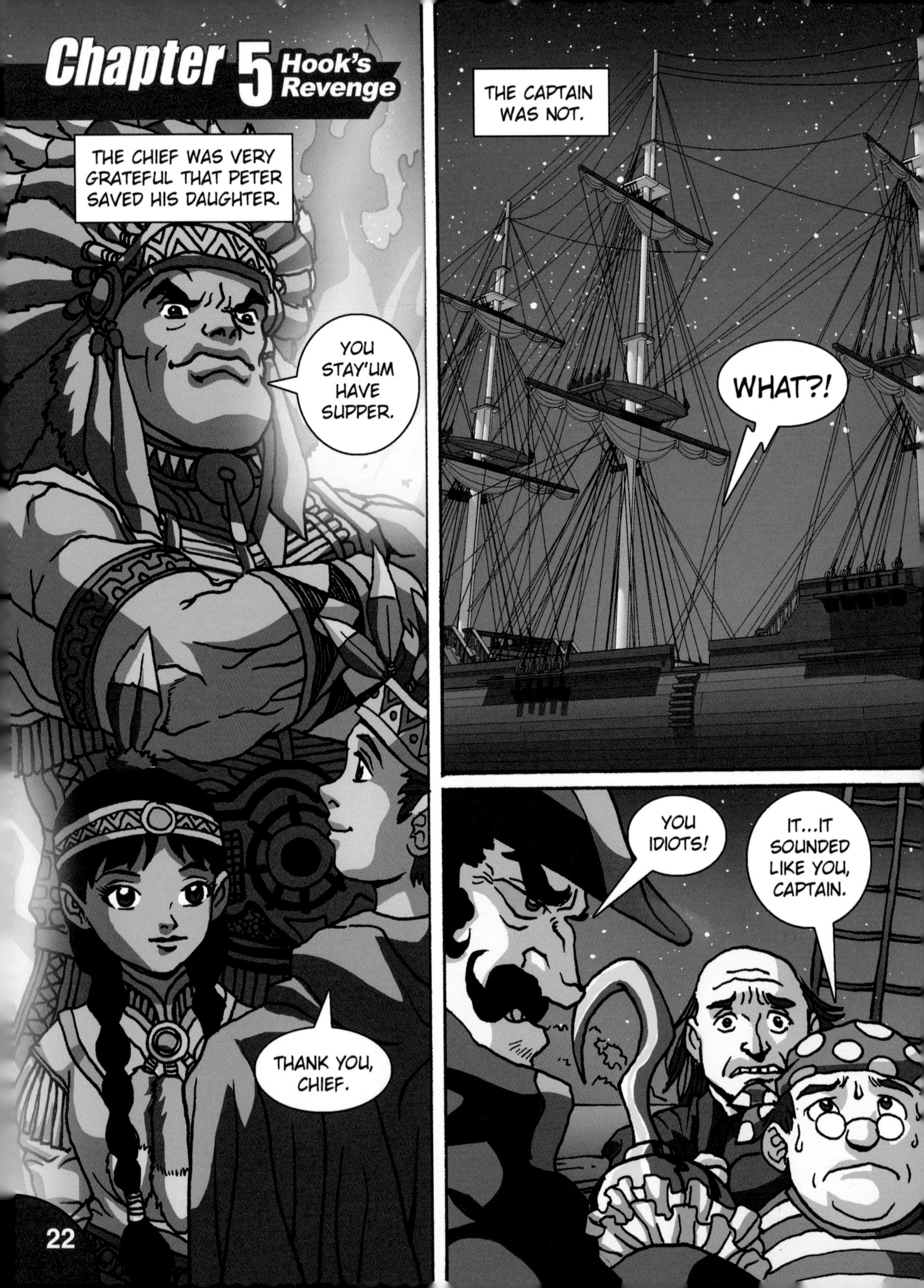
THE CHIEF WAS VERY GRATEFUL THAT PETER SAVED HIS DAUGHTER.
YOU STAY'UM HAVE SUPPER.
THANK YOU, CHIEF.
THE CAPTAIN WAS NOT.
WHAT?!
YOU IDIOTS!
IT...IT SOUNDED LIKE YOU, CAPTAIN.

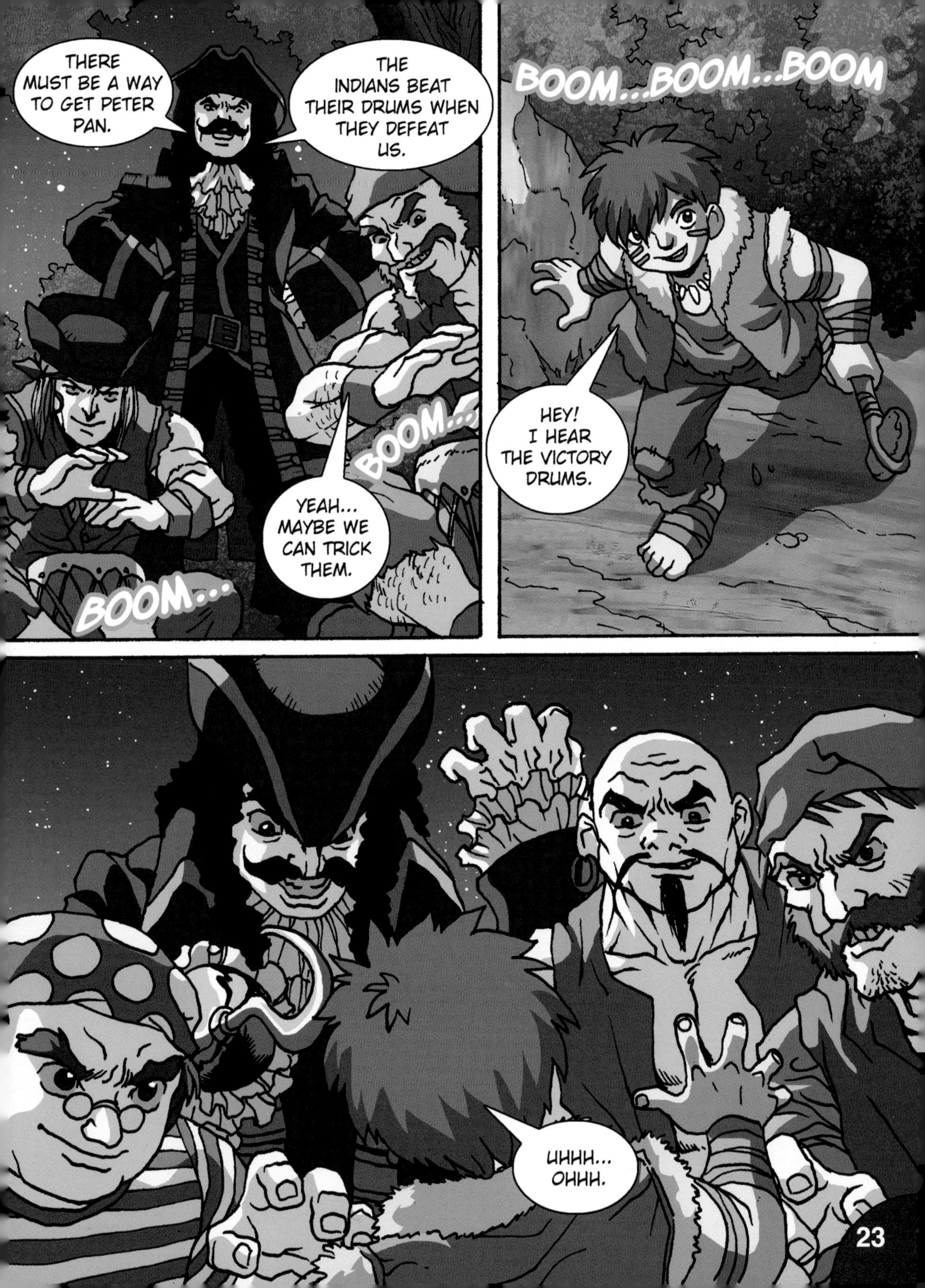
THERE MUST BE A WAY TO GET PETER PAN.
THE INDIANS BEAT THEIR DRUMS WHEN THEY DEFEAT US.
YEAH... MAYBE WE CAN TRICK THEM.
BOOM...
BOOM...
BOOM...BOOM...BOOM
HEY! I HEAR THE VICTORY DRUMS.
UHHH... OHHH.

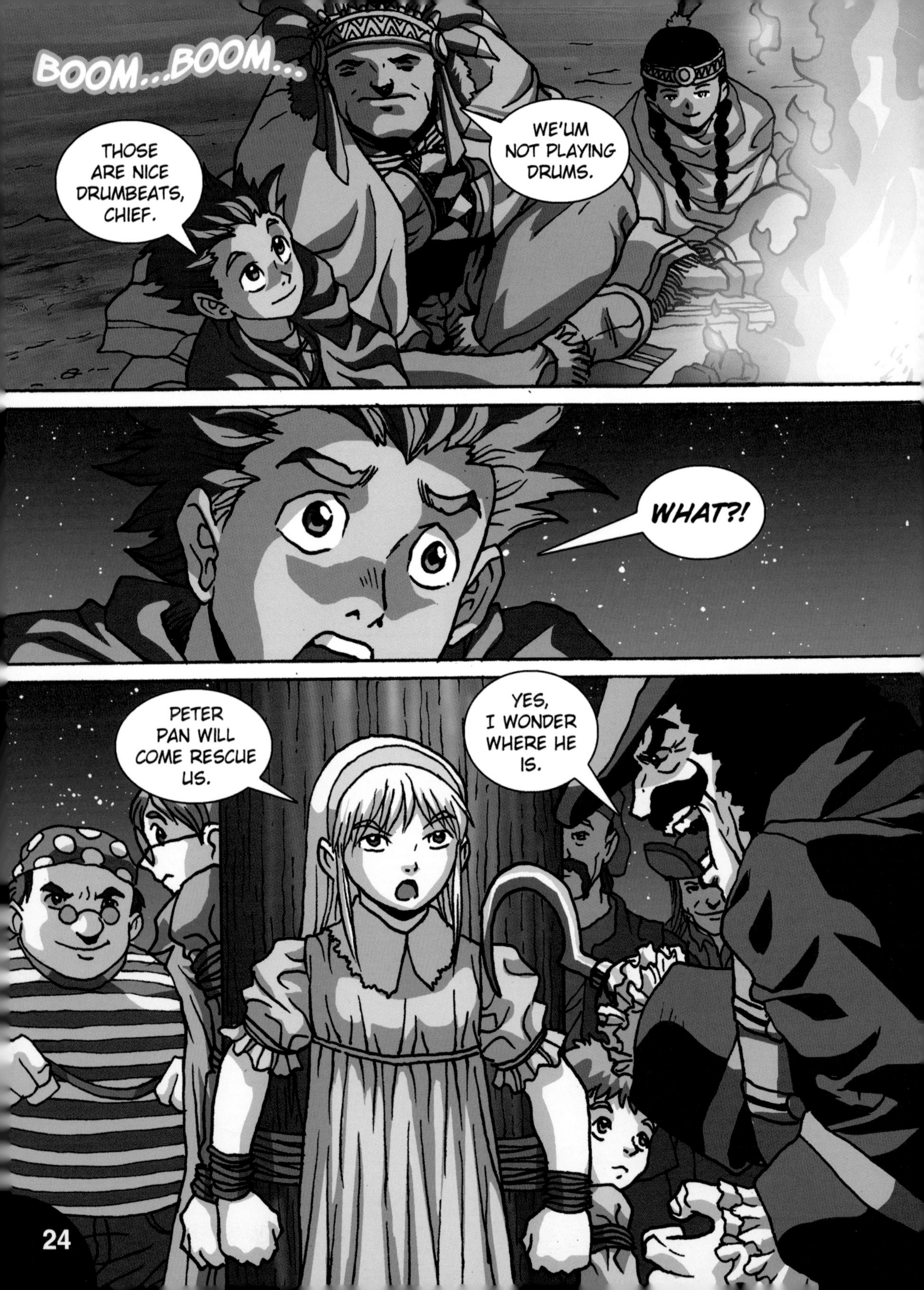
BOOM...BOOM...
THOSE ARE NICE DRUMBEATS, CHIEF.
WE'UM NOT PLAYING DRUMS.
WHAT?!
PETER PAN WILL COME RESCUE US.
YES, I WONDER WHERE HE IS.

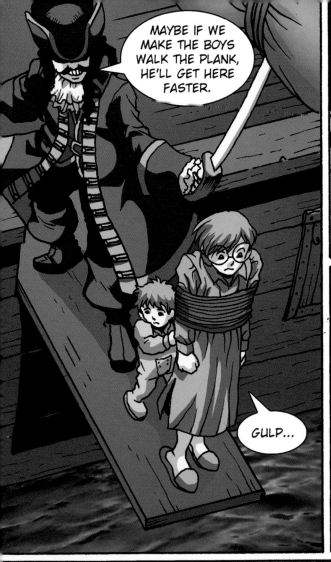

MAYBE IF WE MAKE THE BOYS WALK THE PLANK, HE'LL GET HERE FASTER.

GULP...

TICK TOCK TICK TOCK

IT'S HERE!

HIDE ME!

TICK TOCK TICK TOCK

IT'S NOT THE CROCODILE...

...BUT PETER PAN!

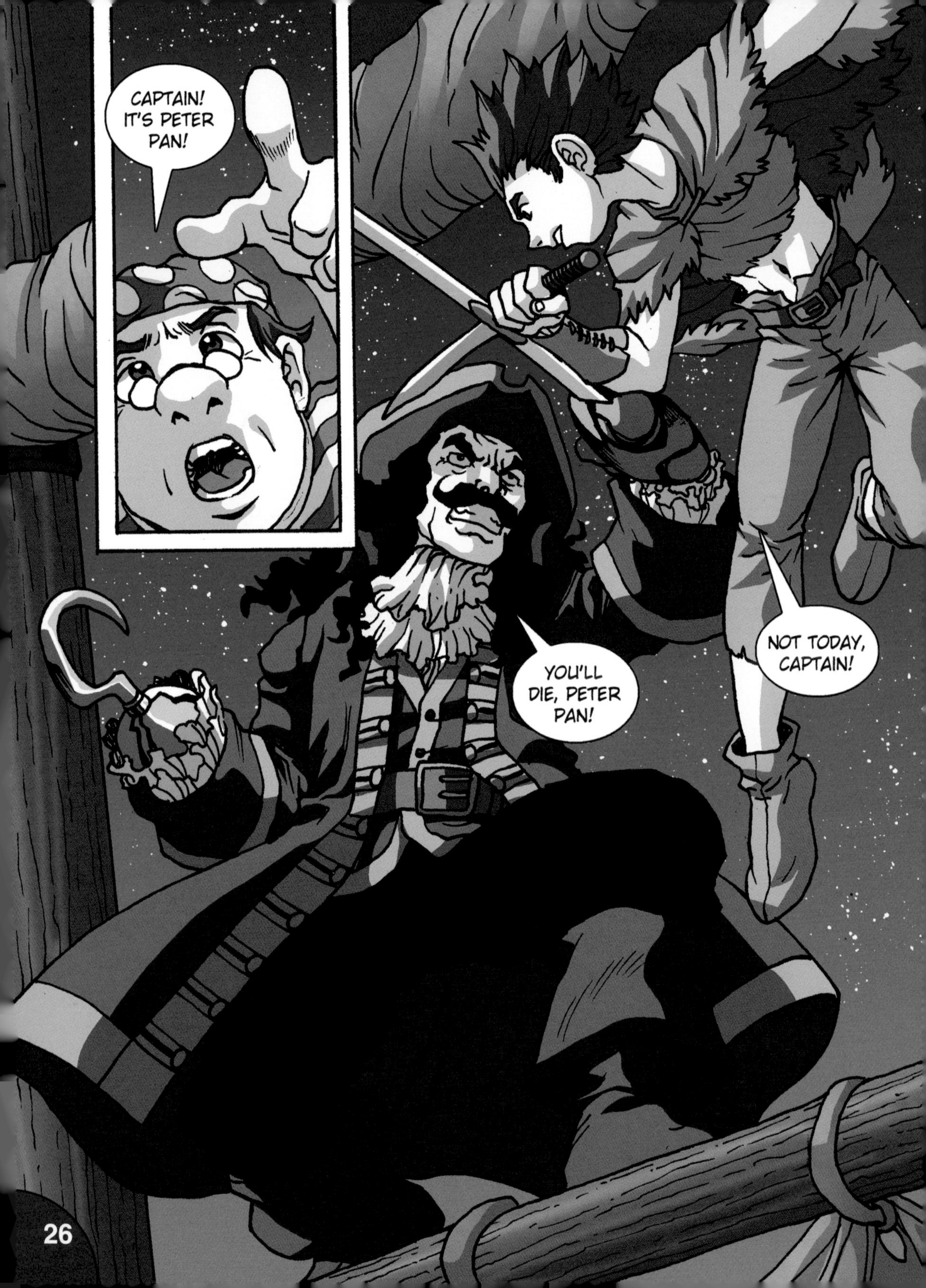
CAPTAIN! IT'S PETER PAN!
YOU'LL DIE, PETER PAN!
NOT TODAY, CAPTAIN!

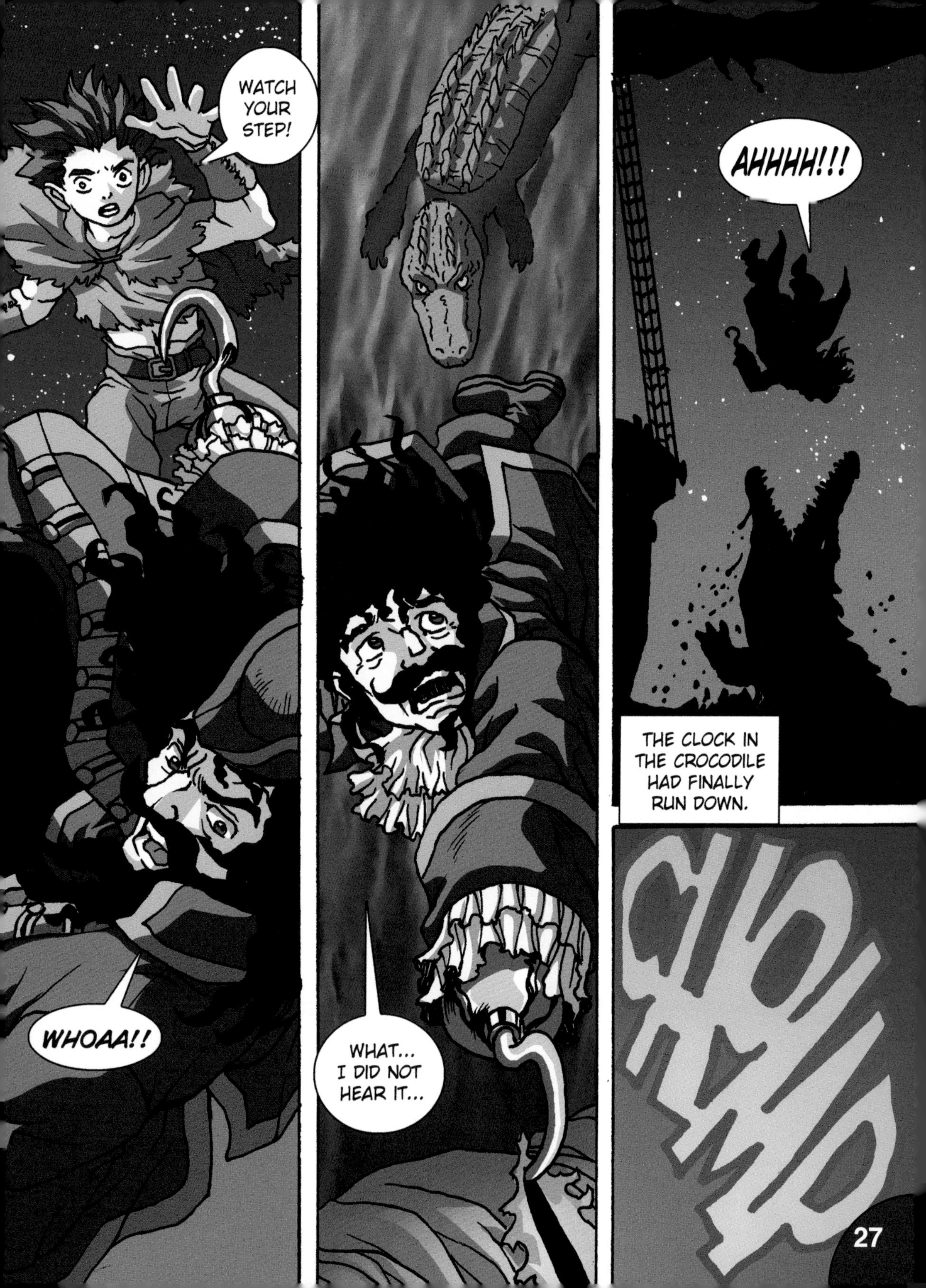
WATCH YOUR STEP!
WHOAA!!
WHAT... I DID NOT HEAR IT...
AHHHH!!!
THE CLOCK IN THE CROCODILE HAD FINALLY RUN DOWN.
CHOMP

Chapter 6 Never Grow Up

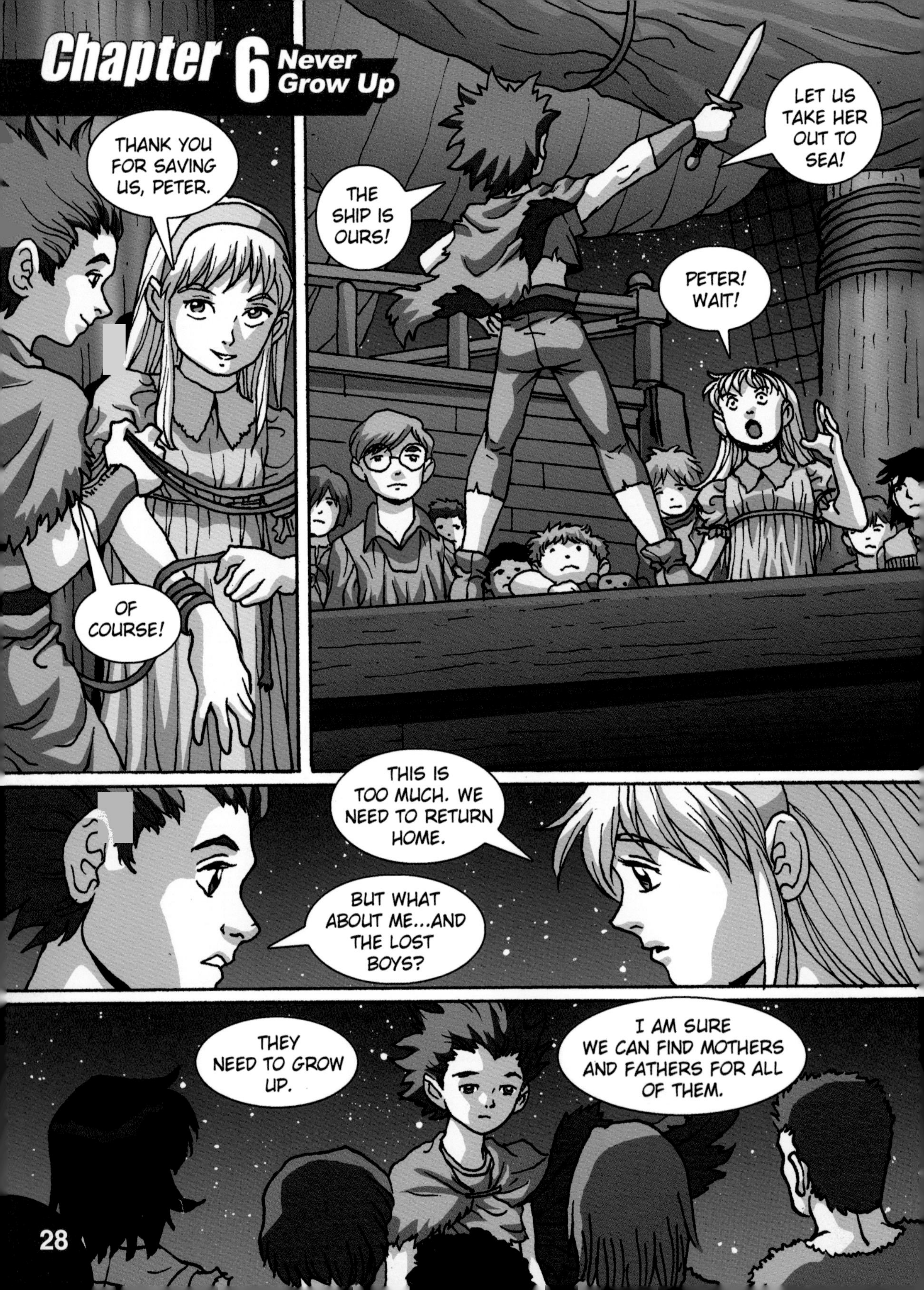
THANK YOU FOR SAVING US, PETER.
OF COURSE!
THE SHIP IS OURS!
LET US TAKE HER OUT TO SEA!
PETER! WAIT!
THIS IS TOO MUCH. WE NEED TO RETURN HOME.
BUT WHAT ABOUT ME...AND THE LOST BOYS?
THEY NEED TO GROW UP.
I AM SURE WE CAN FIND MOTHERS AND FATHERS FOR ALL OF THEM.

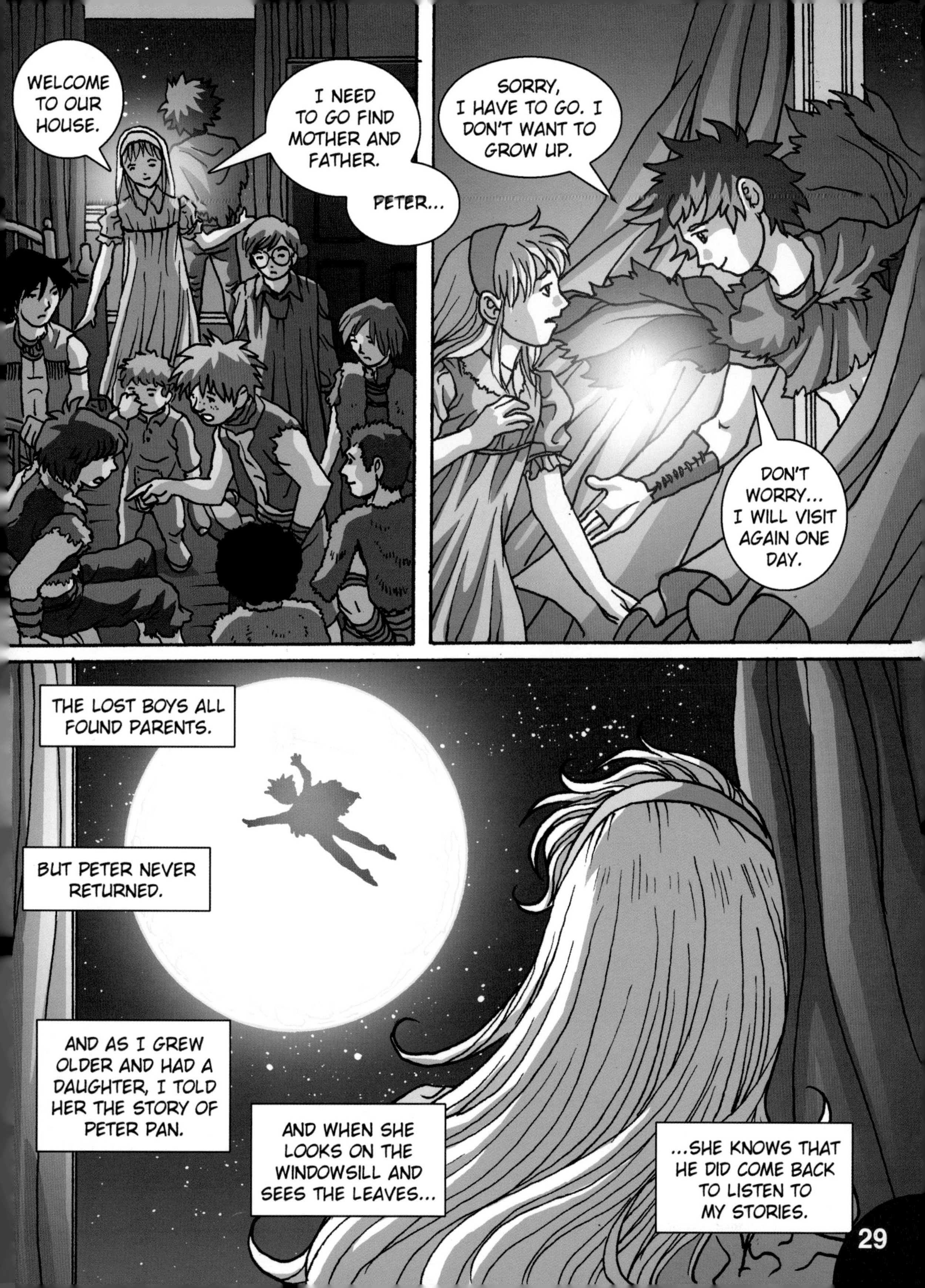
WELCOME TO OUR HOUSE.
I NEED TO GO FIND MOTHER AND FATHER.
PETER...
SORRY, I HAVE TO GO. I DON'T WANT TO GROW UP.
DON'T WORRY... I WILL VISIT AGAIN ONE DAY.
THE LOST BOYS ALL FOUND PARENTS.
BUT PETER NEVER RETURNED.
AND AS I GREW OLDER AND HAD A DAUGHTER, I TOLD HER THE STORY OF PETER PAN.
AND WHEN SHE LOOKS ON THE WINDOWSILL AND SEES THE LEAVES...
...SHE KNOWS THAT HE DID COME BACK TO LISTEN TO MY STORIES.

About the Author

James Matthew Barrie was born in Scotland on May 9, 1860. He was the ninth of ten children to a handloom weaver. At 13, James went to school at Dumfries Academy, where he discovered theater.

From Dumfries Academy, Barrie went to Edinburgh University. He graduated in 1882, and for nearly two years he worked as a journalist. Then in 1885, Barrie moved to London, England, to be a freelance writer.

In 1891, Barrie wrote the best-selling novel *The Little Minister*, which was later turned into a play. After that, Barrie wrote mostly for the theater. He married the actress Mary Ansell in 1894, but had no children.

Barrie and his wife divorced in 1910. He continued to write and work. In 1930, he became the chancellor of Edinburgh University. On June 19, 1937, Barrie died in London. His plays and novels continue to inspire and entertain people around the world.

Additional Works

Additional Works by J.M. Barrie

A Window in Thrums (1888)
The Little Minister (1891)
Sentimental Tommy (1896)
The Little White Bird (1902)
The Admirable Crichton (1902)
Peter Pan (1904)
Dear Brutus (1917)
Mary Rose (1920)

About the Adapter

Joeming Dunn is both a general practice physician and the owner of one of the largest comic companies in Texas, Antarctic Press. A graduate of two Texas schools, Austin College in Sherman and the University of Texas Medical Branch in Galveston, he has currently settled in San Antonio.

Dr. Dunn has written or co-authored texts in both the medical and graphic novel fields. He met his wife, Teresa, in college, and they have two bright and lovely girls, Ashley and Camerin. Ashley has even helped some with his research for these Magic Wagon books.

Glossary

chancellor - the honorary head of a British university.

freelance - of or relating to a person who sells work to anyone who will buy it.

lagoon - a shallow pool of water.

make-believe - a pretending that what is not real is real.

nursemaid - a female hired to look after children.

revenge - an act that is done to get even with another person.

Web Sites

To learn more about J.M. Barrie, visit ABDO Publishing Company on the World Wide Web at **www.abdopublishing.com.** Web sites about Barrie are featured on our Book Links page. These links are routinely monitored and updated to provide the most current information available.